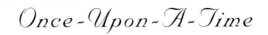

Once-Upon-A-Time

# Three Tales of Trickery

*Little Red Riding Hood*

*Hansel and Gretel*

*Rumpelstiltskin*

Retold by Marilyn Helmer • Illustrated by Noushin Pajouhesh

*Kids Can Press*

*To the Burlington Storytellers' Guild — thank you for the inspiration, the sharing and the friendship — and most of all for those fabulous Friday night stories! — M. H.*

*To Siavash, Soroush and all the kids around the world. — N. P.*

Text © 2002 Marilyn Helmer
Illustrations © 2002 Noushin Pajouhesh

Kids Can Press acknowledges the financial support of the Ontario Arts Council, the Canada Council for the Arts and the Government of Canada, through the BPIDP, for our publishing activity.

Published in Canada by
Kids Can Press Ltd.
29 Birch Avenue
Toronto, ON  M4V 1E2

Published in the U.S. by
Kids Can Press Ltd.
2250 Military Road
Tonawanda, NY  14150

www.kidscanpress.com

The artwork in this book was rendered in gouache.
The text is set in Berkeley.

Series Editor: Debbie Rogosin
Editor: David MacDonald
Design: Marie Bartholomew
Printed in Hong Kong, China, by Wing King Tong Company Limited

This book is smyth sewn casebound.

CM 02  0 9 8 7 6 5 4 3 2 1

**National Library of Canada Cataloguing in Publication Data**

Helmer, Marilyn
        Three tales of trickery

(Once-upon-a-time)
Contents: Hansel and Gretel — Rumpelstiltskin — Little Red Riding Hood.
ISBN 1-55074-937-4

I. Pajouhesh, Noushin, 1968–   II. Title.   III. Series: Helmer, Marilyn. Once-upon-a-time.

PS8565.E4594T473 2002          j398.2          C2001-902827-X
PZ8.H3696Th 2002

Kids Can Press is a *lorus*™ Entertainment Company

# Contents

# Little Red Riding Hood

Once long ago, there was a little girl whose grandmother made her a beautiful red cape with a hood. The little girl put on the cape and declared that she loved it so well, she would wear it forever. From that day on, everyone called her Little Red Riding Hood.

One day, Little Red Riding Hood's mother packed a basket full of cakes and fruit and fresh apple cider. "Grandmother is sick in bed," she said. "This basket of goodies and a visit from you will cheer her up." She handed the basket to Little Red Riding Hood. "Go straight to Grandmother's house, my dear. Stay on the path, don't dawdle and above all do not talk to strangers," she warned.

"Yes, Mama," said Little Red Riding Hood. She waved good-bye and off she ran, down the path that led through the woods to Grandmother's house.

At first Little Red Riding Hood did exactly as she had been told. But the woods were filled with interesting things, and soon she began to dawdle. When she spotted a squirrel, she stopped to feed it some nuts. A bit farther on, she stopped again to watch a robin building its nest. She even sang the robin a song she made up about visiting her grandmother.

But the robin wasn't the only one who heard Little Red Riding Hood. Her song also reached a pair of large hairy ears that were listening nearby. Those ears belonged to a large gray Wolf. Suddenly the Wolf leapt out onto the path, right in front of her!

"Good morning," he said with a friendly smile. "What a pretty basket you have."

"It's full of goodies for my grandmother," said Little Red Riding Hood. "She's sick in bed, and I'm on my way to visit her."

"And where does your grandmother live?" asked the Wolf.

"On the other side of the forest, at the end of this path," said Little Red Riding Hood.

"I know where that is," said the Wolf with a gleam in his eye. "Why don't you take your grandmother a bunch of wildflowers?" he added. "There are some lovely ones growing just beyond that clump of trees." The Wolf pointed with a large hairy paw.

"What a wonderful idea!" exclaimed Little Red Riding Hood. And, forgetting her mother's warning, she left the path and rushed off into the woods to pick flowers.

As soon as Little Red Riding Hood disappeared among the trees, the Wolf headed for Grandmother's house. When he arrived, he knocked on the door.

"Who's there?" Grandmother called out in a frail voice.

"It's Little Red Riding Hood," the Wolf called back sweetly. "I've brought you a basket of goodies."

"Come right in," Grandmother replied.

The Wolf pushed the door open and went straight to the bedroom. Before Grandmother could make a sound, he swallowed her up in one great gulp!

A few moments later there was a knock on the door. Imitating Grandmother's voice, the Wolf called out, "Who's there?"

"It's Little Red Riding Hood," came the reply.

The Wolf noticed a clean nightie and sleeping cap folded on a chair. With a wide wolfish grin, he quickly put on the nightclothes and jumped into Grandmother's bed. "Come in, my dear," he called, pulling the covers right up to his big hairy chin.

Little Red Riding Hood went inside and hurried to the bedroom. But when she saw her Grandmother, she stopped and stared.

"Goodness, Grandmother, what great big eyes you have!" she said.

"All the better to see you with," said the Wolf.

"Goodness, Grandmother, what large hairy ears you have!" exclaimed Little Red Riding Hood.

"All the better to hear you with," said the Wolf.

"And, Grandmother," gasped Little Red Riding Hood, "what long sharp teeth you have!"

"All the better to eat you with!" howled the Wolf. He threw back the covers, sprang from the bed and gobbled up Little Red Riding Hood!

Now the Wolf had never before eaten two big meals in one day. His stomach began to grumble and ache. "Oh-h-h-h!" he groaned, "I must lie down and rest." He flopped onto Grandmother's bed and fell fast asleep.

A short time later, a hunter passed by and heard loud snores coming from Grandmother's house. "Gracious," he exclaimed, "I've never heard the old lady make such a racket. Something must be wrong!"

The hunter hurried inside and looked into the bedroom. Lying on the bed was a large hairy creature wearing a frilly nightie and sleeping cap. A pair of huge hairy feet stuck out from the bottom of the nightie. Two large hairy ears and a great hairy chin poked out from beneath the cap.

"That's no old lady," cried the hunter. "That's a wolf!" He put his rifle to his shoulder and *bang*, that was the end of the Wolf.

The hunter bent over to hoist the Wolf onto his shoulders. Suddenly he jumped back. Something was moving inside the Wolf's belly! The hunter grabbed his knife and cut the Wolf open. Out popped Grandmother and Little Red Riding Hood, alive and well, for the Wolf had swallowed them whole.

Little Red Riding Hood and her Grandmother thanked the hunter over and over again for saving them. Then Grandmother looked into the basket. "There's enough food here for all of us," she said. So the hunter, Little Red Riding Hood and her Grandmother sat down to a fine feast.

When it was time to go, Little Red Riding Hood kissed her Grandmother good-bye. "Go straight home, my dear," said Grandmother. "Stay on the path, don't dawdle and above all do not talk to strangers."

This time Little Red Riding Hood did exactly as she was told, and she arrived safely home in no time.

From that day on, whenever she went to visit her grandmother, Little Red Riding Hood did not dawdle to feed the squirrels or watch the birds. She did not wander off the path to pick wildflowers. And above all, she never spoke to strangers, especially strangers with great big eyes, large hairy ears and long sharp teeth.

# Hansel and Gretel

Once upon a time, at the edge of a great forest, there lived a poor woodcutter with his wife and two children. The boy's name was Hansel and the girl was called Gretel.

One night after the children had gone to bed, the woodcutter turned to his wife. "There is scarcely a morsel of food left in the house," he said. "What are we to do?"

His wife, who was the children's stepmother, said spitefully, "Tomorrow we will take the children deep into the forest and leave them there. They'll never find their way home, so there will be two less mouths to feed."

The woodcutter could hardly believe his ears. "I cannot abandon my beloved children!" he protested.

"Then we will all starve to death," snapped his wife. She nagged and pleaded until, at last, the woodcutter gave in.

All this time, Hansel and Gretel had been crouched together at the top of the stairs, listening to their stepmother's cruel plan. Gretel clung to her brother's arm. "Oh, Hansel, what shall we do?" she whispered.

"Don't worry, Gretel," said Hansel. "I have a plan, too."

After their parents went
to bed, Hansel crept out of
the house. By the light of the
moon, he filled his pockets
with the shiny white pebbles
that lined the path to their cottage.

At dawn, the stepmother shook
Hansel and Gretel awake. "Get up, you pair
of lazybones," she said. "We are going into the forest
to collect wood." The stepmother gave each of the children a dry crust
of bread. "Now come with us and do not lag behind," she said harshly.

Hansel and Gretel followed their parents along the narrow path into
the forest. One by one, Hansel secretly dropped the little white pebbles
from his pocket to mark the way home.

A long time later they stopped by a small brook. The father gathered some branches and built a fire. "This will keep you warm while we go deeper into the forest to chop wood," he said, kissing each child gently on the cheek.

"Stay here until we come back for you," said the stepmother, and she walked quickly away.

For the rest of the afternoon, Hansel and Gretel waited patiently, but their parents did not return. Finally, as the setting sun turned the sky crimson, they ate their bread and fell asleep.

Late that night they awoke to a bright full moon. It shone on the trail of white pebbles, so the children had no trouble finding their way home. When they walked in the door, their father gave a shout of joy. Their stepmother had no words of welcome.

For a while, the family managed. But then the day came when all that was left in the pantry were a few hard rolls. That evening, Hansel and Gretel again overheard their stepmother making plans to get rid of them. Later, when Hansel tried to sneak out to collect more pebbles, he found the door locked and bolted.

In the morning, the stepmother hustled the children out of bed. She gave them each a stale roll and hurried them out the door. This time she made Hansel and Gretel walk in front, so that she could keep an eye on them.

Since Hansel had no pebbles to mark their way, he broke off crumbs from his roll. When his stepmother wasn't looking, he dropped the crumbs along the path until every bit of his bread was gone.

Once again the father built a fire, and he and his wife left Hansel and Gretel alone. When dusk came, Gretel shared her roll with Hansel. Then the two children lay down side by side and went to sleep.

As the moon rose that night, Hansel woke up. "Come, Gretel," he said, nudging his sister awake. "The trail of breadcrumbs will show us the way home." Alas, there was not a breadcrumb to be seen. The birds had eaten every last one.

"Hansel, what are we to going to do?" cried Gretel.

"We'll find our own way back," Hansel said bravely. He reached for Gretel's hand. They walked this way and that, trying to find the path. But all their wandering only led them deeper into the forest. Finally, exhausted, they lay down under a tree and fell fast asleep.

The next morning they were awakened by the sound of a bird singing. "Hansel, look!" said Gretel, pointing to a small white bird flitting over their heads.

Hansel jumped to his feet. "Come, Gretel! I think the bird wants us to follow it." Hand in hand, Hansel and Gretel hurried after the bird. It led them through the trees until they reached a large clearing.

Hansel and Gretel stopped and stared. Ahead was the most extraordinary house they had ever seen. The walls were made of crisp gingerbread, trimmed with fruit drops that sparkled like jewels in the sunlight. The sugar-candy windows were framed with red-and-white peppermint sticks, and the roof was made of plump iced honey-cakes.

With shouts of delight, the children ran toward the house. Gretel helped herself to a peppermint stick and a handful of fruit drops. Hansel broke off a chunk of gingerbread and took a big bite.

Suddenly, they were startled by a voice calling:

> *What do I hear? A little mouse?*
> *Nibbling, nibbling at my house?*

The cottage door flew open and out hobbled an old woman. Hansel and Gretel turned to run, but the old woman spoke gently:

> *Darling children, do not fear;*
> *My sight is poor, so please come near.*
> *Inside you'll find a special treat*
> *Of more delicious things to eat.*

The old woman sounded so kind that Hansel and Gretel followed her inside. Little did they know that she was really a witch in disguise! The minute Hansel and Gretel stepped over the threshold, the Witch slammed the door. In a flash she grabbed Hansel, shoved him into a cage and locked it.

From that day on, the Witch kept Gretel busy cooking rich tasty meals for Hansel. While he ate, the Witch cackled:

> *I'll make you fatter, never thinner,*
> *And very soon you'll be my dinner!*

Every morning the Witch made Hansel stick a finger between the bars of his cage to see how fat he'd grown. But Hansel was too clever for her. Instead of his finger, he stuck out an old chicken bone. The Witch's eyesight was so poor that she thought the bone was Hansel's finger. She couldn't understand why Hansel never grew any fatter.

Finally the Witch lost her patience. She screamed at Gretel:

*Light the fire and heat the pot;*
*I'll eat your brother, fat or not!*

Trembling with fear, Gretel did as she was told. When the fire in the oven was blazing, the Witch ordered Gretel to see if it was hot enough. As Gretel turned toward the oven, she noticed the Witch creeping up behind her. Fearing what the Witch might do, Gretel stepped aside. "How can I tell if it's hot enough?" she asked.

In reply the Witch shrieked:

*A foolish girl I can't abide.*
*Open the door and crawl inside!*

She leaned into the oven to show Gretel what to do. At that moment, Gretel reached into the Witch's pocket and grabbed the key to the cage. With a mighty push, she sent the Witch headfirst into the hot oven. Gretel slammed the door shut and that was the end of the Witch. Then Gretel rushed to unlock Hansel's cage and the two hugged each other joyfully.

Beyond the kitchen was a room the Witch had never allowed Gretel to enter. Curious, Hansel and Gretel opened the door and peeked inside. To their amazement, they found trunks and chests overflowing with precious jewels.

"We can take these home to Father!" exclaimed Hansel.

"We'll be rich!" declared Gretel. They quickly filled their pockets with treasure and set out for home.

On their way through the forest, Hansel and Gretel came to a great lake. "How will we ever get across?" cried Hansel.

"Look!" said Gretel. She pointed to a beautiful white swan gliding toward them. "Perhaps it will carry us to the other side." And indeed the swan did.

When Hansel and Gretel were safely across the lake, they thanked the swan. Then they set off through the forest once again. Soon the rocks and streams began to look more and more familiar. Suddenly Hansel spotted an opening in the trees ahead. "It's the path to our cottage!" he cried.

Before they knew it, Hansel and Gretel were running into their father's arms. He wept with joy to see his beloved children safely home. "Your stepmother is dead," he told them. "I have searched the forest every day, hoping to find you."

"Now we can live together in peace," said Hansel.

"And we will never be hungry again," said Gretel as she danced around the room, showering them with the jewels from her pockets.

From that day on, the children and their father lived happily in the little cottage near the edge of the forest. The pantry was always full, and if they haven't moved away, they are living there still.

# Rumpelstiltskin

There once was a poor miller who loved to boast and brag. When he chanced to meet the King one day, the miller quickly thought of a way to impress him. "Your Majesty," he declared, "I have a beautiful daughter who is so clever that she can spin straw into gold."

"What a remarkable talent!" exclaimed the King, who was very fond of gold. "Bring your daughter to my palace by sundown tomorrow. If she is as clever as you say, she will be very useful to me."

As soon as the girl arrived, the King led her into a room filled with straw. A large spinning wheel stood in the corner. "Spin this straw into gold by morning," he ordered. "If you fail, you will not live to see another day." Then the King left the room, locking the door behind him.

The miller's daughter burst into tears. "What am I to do?" she sobbed. "I know nothing about spinning straw into gold."

Suddenly the door flew open and a strange little man danced into the room. He stood before the miller's daughter and said:

> *Tell me, tell me, maiden fair,*
> *Why are you in such despair?*

"The King has ordered me to spin this straw into gold," replied the girl, "but I have not the faintest idea how to do it."

The little man smiled and said:

> *Do not despair; I'll do your task.*
> *A just reward is all I ask.*

"I'll give you my necklace," said the girl. The little man took the necklace and sat down at the spinning wheel.

*Whir, whir, whir.* The wheel spun round and round. As the miller's daughter watched in amazement, the spools filled with gold thread. By sunrise the job was done, and the little man disappeared.

When the King saw the gold, he was very pleased. But was he satisfied? Not on your life!

That evening he led the girl into a larger room filled with straw. "Remember my warning," he said. "Spin this straw into gold by morning or you will die." With that he walked out, locking the door behind him.

Once again the miller's daughter burst into tears. As quickly as before, the strange little man appeared and said:

> *Do not despair; I'll do your task.*
> *A just reward is all I ask.*

"I'll give you my ring," said the girl. The little man took the ring and sat down at the spinning wheel.

*Whir, whir, whir.* The wheel spun round and round, and the spools filled with gold thread. By dawn the job was done. Before the miller's daughter could so much as say "Thank you!" the little man disappeared.

When the King saw the second room filled with gold he was delighted. But was he satisfied? Not on your life!

"This girl may be only a miller's daughter, but she is worth her weight in gold," the King said to himself. He took her by the hand and led her into a third room filled with straw. This room was even larger than the one before. "Spin this straw into gold by morning," he said. "If you do, you will be my bride."

The girl was more distraught than ever. Again the strange little man appeared and said:

> *Do not despair; I'll do your task.*
> *A just reward is all I ask.*

"I have nothing left to give you," sobbed the girl.

"Then promise me your first-born child," said the little man.

The girl stared at him, aghast. "I have no choice but to agree," she thought, "for if the straw is not spun into gold by morning, I will surely lose my life." And so she gave her promise.

*Whir, whir, whir.* The wheel spun round and round, and the spools filled with gold thread. By daybreak the job was done and the room was aglitter with gold. Then, just as before, the little man disappeared.

At the sight of the third room filled with gold, the King was finally satisfied. "Now you will be my Queen," he said to the miller's daughter, and they were married the next day.

The miller's daughter was so content to be Queen that she forgot all about the strange little man. A year later, to her great joy, she gave birth to a beautiful baby. But the Queen's joy was short-lived, for the very next day the little man appeared to claim the child.

The Queen wept and begged for mercy. She offered the little man all the riches of the kingdom if he would let her keep the child. Finally her sorrow touched his heart, and the little man said:

*Three days you have to guess my name;*
*Succeed, and I'll give up my claim.*
*But if you fail within that time,*
*Your precious child will then be mine.*

That night the Queen lay awake, trying to remember all the names she had ever heard. At dawn she rose and paced the floor, dreading the moment when the little man would appear. When he did, she asked hopefully, "Is your name Caspar?"

"No!" said the little man.

"Melchior?"

"No!"

"Balthazar?"

"No!"

As the Queen continued guessing one name after another, the little man cried, "No!" to each one. Finally he skipped off singing:

> *Just two more days to guess my name,*
> *Or your sweet child is mine to claim!*

That evening the Queen sent servants throughout the land to collect the most unusual names they could find. All night long she sat by the window, waiting for the servants to return. As each one did, he reported the names he had found.

When the little man appeared the next day, the Queen asked, "Is your name Barleywort?"

"No!" said the little man.

"Glumgullet?"

"No!"

"Shimmyshanks?"

"No!" cried the little man.

The Queen tried all the names the servants had found. With whoops of delight, the little man shouted "No!" to each one. Then he skipped away singing:

*Just one more day to guess my name,*
*Or your sweet child is mine to claim!*

One servant had not yet returned from the search. He was the Queen's last hope. Finally, just before dawn on the third day, the Queen heard his horse approach the castle door. She rushed to him and pleaded, "Please, tell me what names you have found."

The servant replied, "In a small clearing in a distant forest, I saw a strange little man dancing around a fire singing:

*Today I brew, tomorrow I bake,*
*And then the Queen's dear child I'll take.*
*She'll never win this guessing game*
*For Rumpelstiltskin is my name."*

The Queen was overjoyed. "You have served me well," she said, and she rewarded the servant with a bag of gold.

When the little man appeared
the next morning, the Queen
asked, "Is your name John?"

"No!" said the little man.

"Harry?"

"No!"

"Then could it be ... Rumpelstiltskin?"

"A witch told you that! A witch told you that!" screamed the little man. His face flushed red as fire. He spun about in such a rage that he turned himself into a whirlwind. With a whoosh he flew out the window and the Queen never again laid eyes on the strange little man who could spin straw into gold.